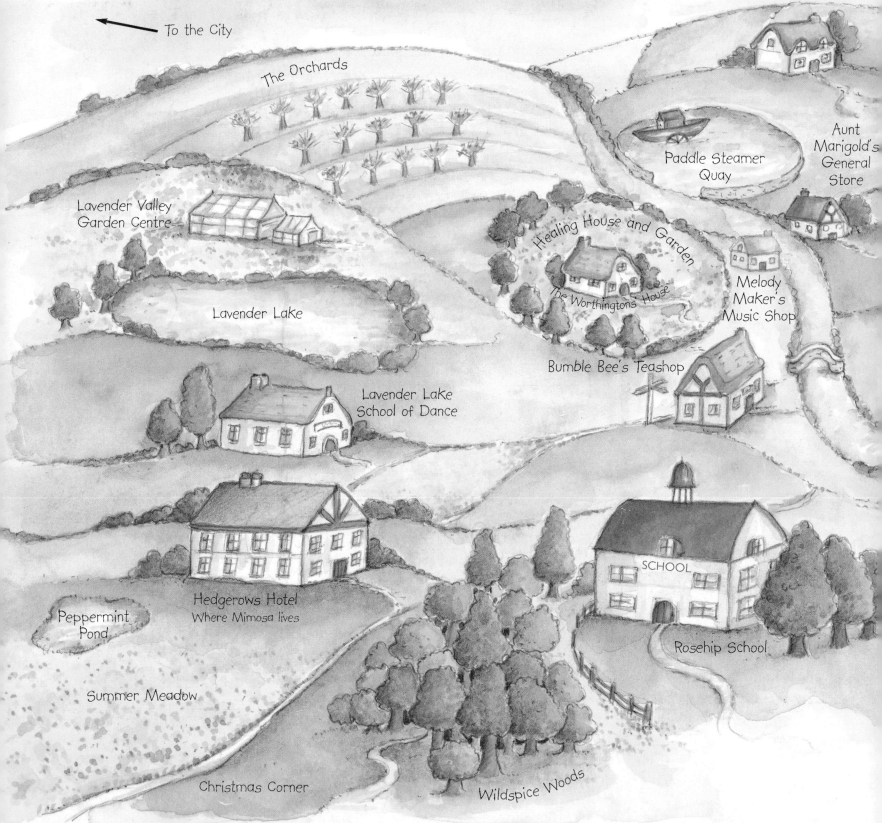

Visit Princess Poppy for fun, games, puzzles,
activities, downloads and lots more at:

www.princesspoppy.com

THE ROYAL PARADE
A PICTURE CORGI BOOK 978 0 552 56561 5

First published in Great Britain by Picture Corgi,
an imprint of Random House Children's Books
A Random House Group Company

This edition published 2012

1 3 5 7 9 10 8 6 4 2

Text copyright © Janey Louise Jones, 2012
Illustration copyright © Picture Corgi Books, 2012
Illustrations by Veronica Vasylenko
The right of Janey Louise Jones and Veronica Vasylenko to be identified as the author and illustrator of this work has been
asserted in accordance with the Copyright, Designs and Patents Act 1988.

www.**princesspoppy**.com
www.**kids**at**random house**.co.uk
www.**random house**.co.uk

Addresses for companies within The Random House Group Limited can be found at: www.randomhouse.co.uk/offices.htm

THE RANDOM HOUSE GROUP Limited Reg. No. 954009

A CIP catalogue record for this book is available from the British Library.

Printed in China

The Royal Parade

Written by Janey Louise Jones

PICTURE CORGI

Especially for (Princess) Elfie (Gleeson),
who loves to dress up, just like Princess Poppy

The Royal Parade

featuring

Mum

Saffron

Princess Poppy

Farmer
Meadowsweet

Honey

David

Granny
Bumble

The Honeypot Hill dress-up parade and street party was a week away. This year the theme was royalty. Poppy and Honey were so excited.

"I'm going to dress up as a royal princess," announced Poppy as they looked through her mum's old dressing-up box.

"I'm going to be a queen," said Honey.

They carried a bundle of dressing-up clothes down to Poppy's bedroom to have a better look.

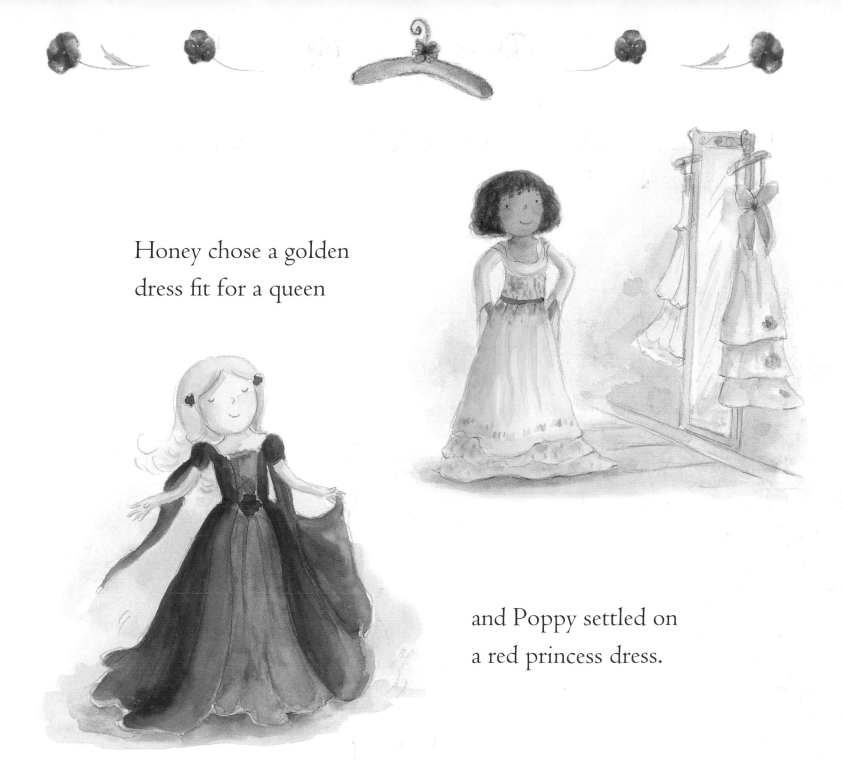

Honey chose a golden
dress fit for a queen

and Poppy settled on
a red princess dress.

Both were gorgeous but rather shabby.
"I know!" exclaimed Poppy. "Let's ask Saffron to mend them."

"Where are you two going?" asked Mum. "Aren't you coming to the
Village Hall? Granny Bumble is giving out jobs for the parade."

Poppy was so excited about her costume that it had slipped her mind.

When they arrived at the hall it was packed. Everyone wanted to help.

Granny Bumble read out her list.

Bumble Bee's Teashop

Granny Bumble's party List

Sandwiches   Mrs Turner
and
Sweetpea

Drinks   Lavender and Marigold

Cakes   Me and Honey

Tables and Chairs   Grandpa

Music   Mr + Mrs Melody + Abigail

Decorations   Saffron

Honeypot Hill Olympics   David

Parade Cart   Farmer Meadowsweet

Medals for races   Holly Mallow

There was a lot to do. But Poppy wasn't down for anything.
She was very disappointed.

"I need help with the parade cart," said Farmer Meadowsweet.

"I'll do it!" Poppy offered.

"Grand!" he replied. "It'll need cleaning and decorating. You can be in charge of that and I'll get Hermione groomed."

Poppy was thrilled to have such an important job. The cart led the parade every year.

That night Poppy took ages to get to sleep and her dreams were filled with thoughts of the parade.

The next day she felt very tired so she decided to take things easy.

Poppy didn't go to Barley Farm.

On Monday morning Poppy and Honey went to Saffron's Sewing
Shop with their dresses.

They chose new
sequins and ribbons,

and picked out some
regal accessories.

Then Saffron pinned
up their hems.

After a while Saffron explained that she had to make bunting for the parade and that she would finish their costumes later in the week.

"Oh, that reminds me," said Poppy. "I must wash the cart."

She thanked Saffron, said goodbye to Honey and skipped off towards Barley Farm.

As Poppy wandered through the village, day-dreaming about her costume, she bumped into David, who was going to mark out tracks for the Honeypot Hill Olympics.

"Can I help?" said Poppy. She decided she would go to the farm later.

"Of course," replied David.

Poppy didn't make it to Barley Farm that day either.

On Tuesday Poppy set off for the farm nice and early. She met Saffron on the way.

"Hi, Poppy," Saffron called. "I've almost finished your costume. Would you like to come and have a look?"

"Oh, yes please!" Poppy replied, desperate to see it.

She would wash the cart straight afterwards, she decided.

The village bustled with activity and the week flashed by.

Mum and Aunt Marigold squeezing lemons

Saffron sewing away

Honey and her granny baking

The Melodys hard at work

On Saturday morning Poppy awoke with a start. The phone was ringing.
It was the day of the parade. But she didn't feel excited. She
felt worried.

"That was Farmer Meadowsweet!" called Mum. "He isn't happy.
He wants you to go to the farm. Now."

Mum was right. Farmer Meadowsweet was not happy and Poppy knew why. She *had* meant to do her job but other things had got in the way.

"We'll have to cancel the parade!" said the farmer crossly.

"I'm sorry," sobbed Poppy. "I really did mean to do it but there was so much other stuff happening. I'll do it right now."

Farmer Meadowsweet tutted doubtfully, quite sure it wouldn't be ready in time.

Although he was angry and disappointed, the farmer saw how sorry Poppy was and how much she wanted to fix things, so he offered to help.

Poppy worked as she had never worked before. She was determined not to ruin the parade.

But they were running out of time . . .

At two o'clock the parade began.

Poppy and her friends, dressed in their royal finery, stood in the beautifully decorated cart as Hermione pulled it through Honeypot Hill.

The other villagers followed.

There was clapping and cheering, tooting and hooting, music, balloons, bunting and streamers.

When the parade ended it was time for the street party!
Poppy dashed over to help.

She finished setting the tables,

laid out the sandwiches,

put a cupcake at each place

and poured the lemonade.

Everyone tucked in.
It was deeeelicious!

After tea the Honeypot Hill Olympics kicked off!

The egg-and-spoon race was funny, the three-legged race was hilarious, and throwing the beanbag in the hoop was a giggle! But the best thing of all was that Poppy was chosen to give out the prizes!

"Poppy, you were a very helpful Parade Princess . . . in the end!"
chuckled Farmer Meadowsweet when the races were over.
"That truly was a grand parade!"

Poppy beamed and promised herself that she would never let things
get in the way like that again.